USBORNE FIRST READING

# Polar Bears

Conrad Mason
Illustrated by Daniel Howarth

# Dragon

Based on the story by Kenneth Grahame
Illustrated by Fred Blunt

USBORNE FIRST READING

# Why the Sea is Salty

Retold by Rosie Dickins
Illustrated by Sara Rojo

USBORNE FIRST READING

# Thumbelina

Retold by
Susanna Davidson
Illustrated by Petra Brown

# The Story of Baby Jesus

### Retold by Mary Kelly

## Illustrated by John Joven

Reading consultant: Alison Kelly
Roehampton University

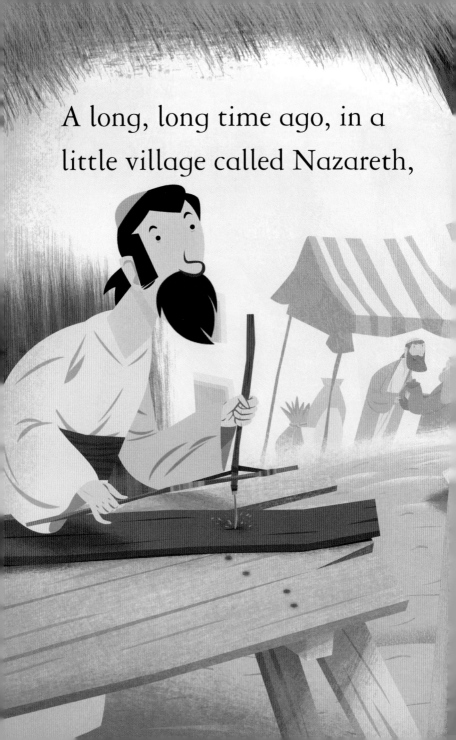

A long, long time ago, in a little village called Nazareth,

there lived a young
couple named Mary
and Joseph.

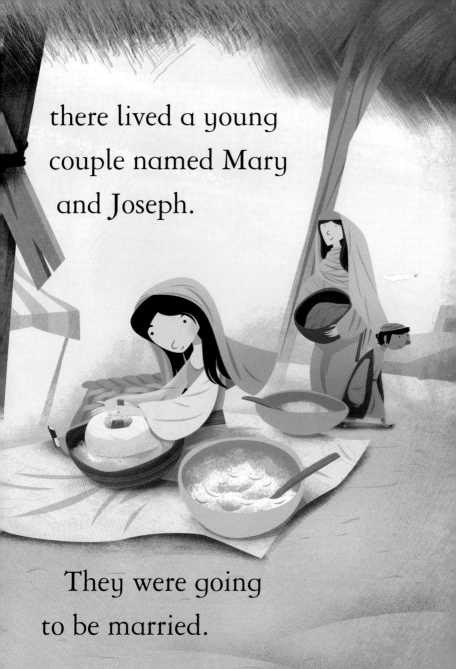

They were going
to be married.

One day, an angel came to Mary. He was dressed in shining white.

"Don't be afraid," he said.

"God has sent me to tell you that you are going to have a baby."

"You must call him
Jesus. He will be
the Son of God."

Mary trembled with fear.

She knelt before the angel.
"I am God's servant," she
said. "I will do as He wishes."

Mary went straight to
Joseph, to tell him the news.

He didn't know what to think.

That night, he had a dream.
An angel appeared before him.

"Mary is having God's
son," said the angel. "He will
help people everywhere."

Soon after, Mary and Joseph were married.

"I'll take care of you and the baby," Joseph promised.

Then the rulers of the land
passed a new law.

Everyone had to go back
to the place where they were
born, to pay a special tax.

11

"We must go to Bethlehem," Joseph told Mary. "It's many miles away."

They loaded up their donkey with food and clothes.

Together, they set out on
the long journey.

They walked over the
green hills of Galilee...

...all the way to Bethlehem.

They arrived as the sun was
setting. Mary felt tired as they
crossed the crowded streets.

Joseph knocked on door
after door, trying to find a
place to stay.

"We're full!" said
the innkeepers.

At the last inn, the innkeeper shook his head.

"I have no room left at my inn," he said. "But you can sleep in the stable if you like."

Joseph made Mary
a bed out of straw.

22

That night, the
baby was born.
23

Mary wrapped him in a
swaddling cloth...

...and laid him in a manger
full of hay.

On the hills outside
Bethlehem, some shepherds
were watching their sheep.

An angel appeared, bright
gold against the night sky.
"Don't be afraid," he said.

27

"Go to Bethlehem.
There you will
find a baby in
a manger."

"He is the Son of God."

Above them, the night
sky filled with angels.

Peace on earth

The angels
gave thanks to God.

They sang beautiful songs
to welcome the new baby
into the world.

Glory to God

The shepherds rushed to
the stable. They knelt in
front of baby Jesus.

They were filled with joy.

The shepherds told
Mary what the
angel had said.

She looked at her
baby in wonder.

33

The shepherds walked through Bethlehem, telling everyone about baby Jesus.

Far away, in the East, some
Wise Men saw a bright star.

They had studied the
stars for many years.

They knew this star
meant something amazing
had happened.

37

For many days and nights
they rode across the desert,
always following the star.

Until, at last, it brought
them to the little town of
Bethlehem.

They gave Mary the
presents they had brought
with them –

gold,

frankincense

and myrrh.

Then they knelt down and worshipped baby Jesus.

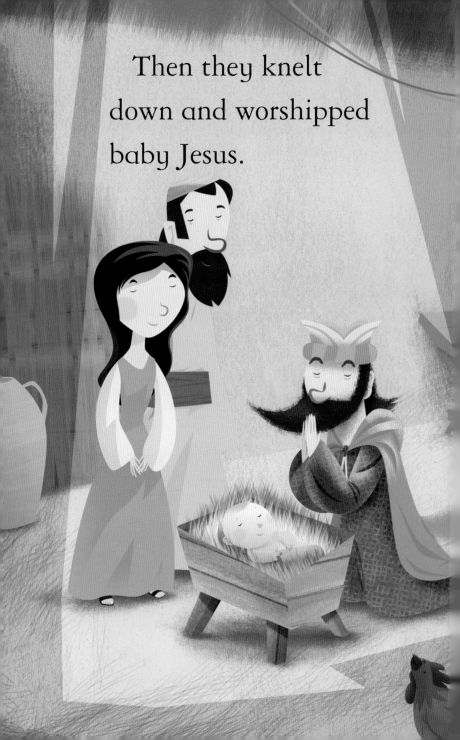

It took Mary and Joseph
a long time to reach
home again.

The journey was hard, but they were filled with hope.

They knew that their baby would grow up to do great and wonderful things.

# USBORNE FIRST READING
## Level Four

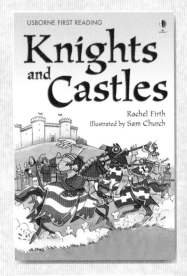

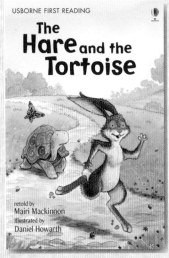